MW01093227

SID AND THE MINI-SLOTHS

WRITTEN BY JENNIFER FRANTZ
ILLUSTRATIONS BY ARTFUL DOODLERS, UK

HarperKidsEntertainment
An Imprint of HarperCollinsPublishers

ICE AGE 2: SID AND THE MINI-SLOTHS

Ice Age 2 The Meltdown ™ & © 2006 Twentieth Century Fox Film Corporation. All rights reserved.

HarperCollins®, ®, and HarperKidsEntertainment™
are trademarks of HarperCollins Publishers.
Printed in the U.S.A.
No part of this book may be used or reproduced in any manner whatsoever
without written permission except in the case of brief quotations embodied in critical articles and reviews.
For information address HarperCollins Children's Books, a division of HarperCollins Publishers,
1350 Avenue of the Americas, New York, NY 10019.
Library of Congress catalog card number: 2005928971
www.harperchildrens.com
www.iceage2.com

First Edition

The glaciers had begun to melt—
and that meant a big flood was on the way!
All the animals in the valley were trying to outrun it,
and Diego, Manny, and Sid were no different.

Exhausted from the day's travels, the friends set up a campfire and lay down for some rest.

The campfire was beginning to fade.
Sid was sleeping peacefully on a rock
when suddenly—the rock started to move!
As Sid slumbered on, he was carried off
into the forest by a group of mini-sloths.

Sid awoke startled and confused. Staring back at him was a whole village of mini-sloths! The mini-sloths dropped to their knees and bowed down to a very puzzled Sid.

Then one of the mini-sloths led Sid over to a giant sculpture, which, strangely, looked a lot like him. "Fire-god make fire," the mini-sloth commanded, handing Sid two stones.

Not wanting to disappoint his new fans, Sid rubbed the two rocks together, creating a spark. "Let there be fire!" he called out at the top of his voice, hoping to impress the crowd.

As fire burned around the bottom of the sculpture, the mini-sloths gave a triumphant cry.

Sid was beginning to think that being a Fire-god was pretty cool.
He posed.
He danced.
He waved.

But soon things were not looking so good for Sid the Fire-god.

Like the other animals, the mini-sloths had noticed that the ice was melting. And they had come up with their own solution to the problem—to sacrifice the Fire-god. That meant Sid!

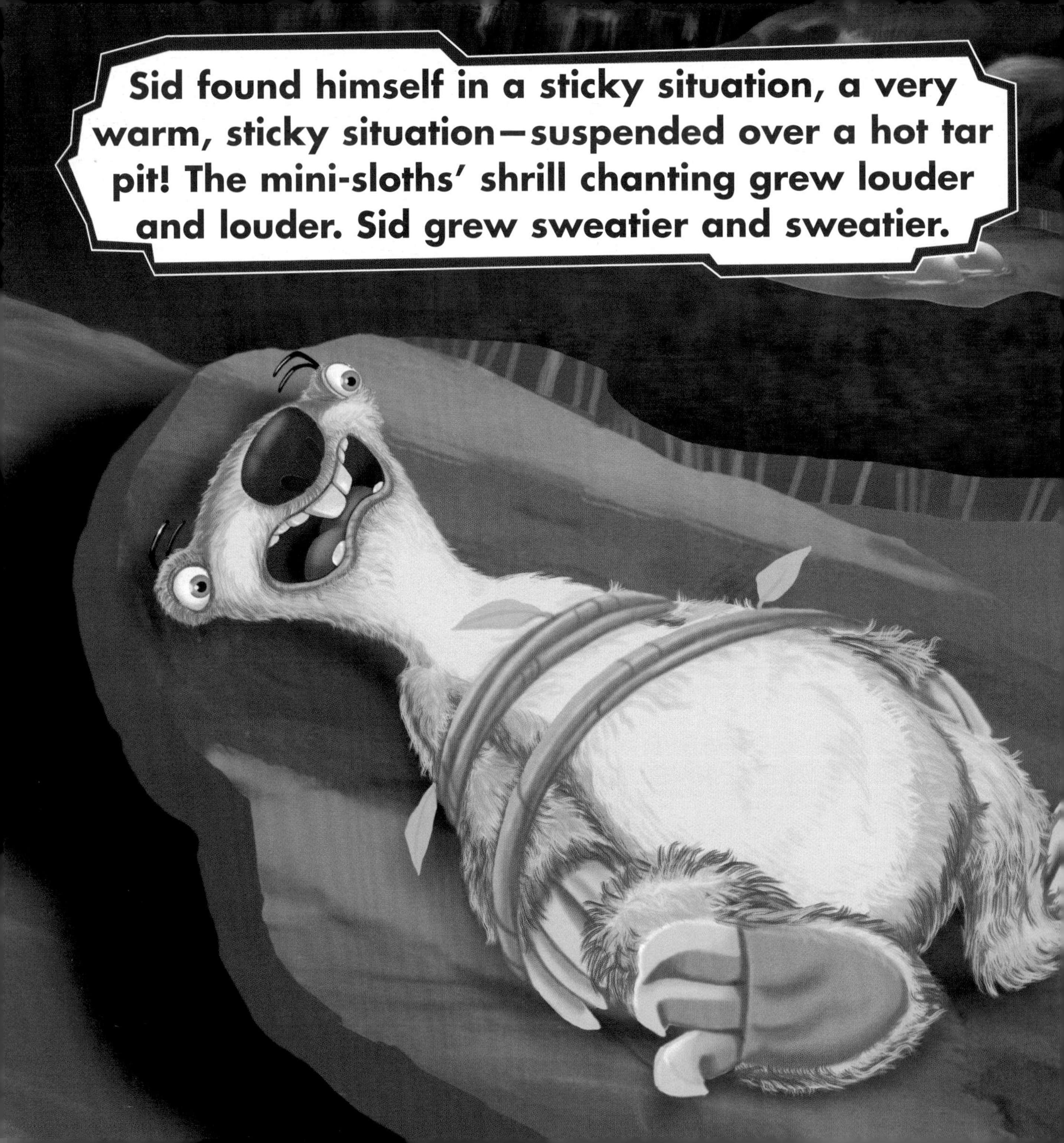
Sid found himself in a sticky situation, a very warm, sticky situation—suspended over a hot tar pit! The mini-sloths' shrill chanting grew louder and louder. Sid grew sweatier and sweatier.

Then suddenly the sloths flung Sid into the pit. He let out a scream as he hurtled straight toward the bubbling tar.

But Sid was lucky! One of the vines he was tied with caught on a rock. Then it started to unravel, but just when Sid was about to sink into the tar, the stretchy vine snapped him back up like a yo-yo.

The mini-sloths cheered when Sid's head poked back up above the pit. But then he started down again and this time, the cord snapped him up a second too late. Sid was covered in tar. Bones from the bottom of the pit were stuck all over his fur!

When the vine tossed him out of the pit this time, looking very different, the mini-sloths thought he was a terrible monster. They ran away when Sid landed on the head of the giant sculpture of himself.

Free of the mini-sloths, Sid was just starting to relax when bats flew out of the sculpture's nose. He was busy swatting them away when all of a sudden the statue crumbled and Sid went tumbling head over heels down a hill. The next thing he knew, Sid was seeing stars. Then everything went very, very blurry, and Sid began to feel very, very sleepy.

Sid's friends were just starting to wonder where he was when they heard a familiar sound. "That's Sid's voice!" Manny called to the others. Then the sloth himself came into sight, conked out on a log that was floating downstream.

Manny nudged his friend with his trunk.
"I am the Fire-god. Kneel before me!"
Sid responded, still sleeping.
"Sid, wake up!" Manny cried,
giving him a strange look.

When he came to, Sid told his friends all about his adventures—being kidnapped, *and* worshipped by mini-sloths, *and* thrown into a hot tar pit.

Manny and Diego were suspicious of Sid's story. "You were sleepwalking," Diego told him. Manny agreed that clearly it was all just a dream.

Even if his friends didn't believe him, Sid knew he'd had an exciting adventure as the Fire-god. But now he was happy to be back where he belonged . . . and back to being plain old Sid.